P9-DNO-015

ELLSWOR
EXTRAOR
ELECTRIC

BY VALORIE FISHER

TH'S Dinary ears

and other
amazing
alphabet
anecdotes

AN ANNE SCHWARTZ BOOK
Atheneum Books for Young Readers
New York   London   Toronto   Sydney   Singapore

Atheneum Books for Young Readers

An imprint of Simon & Schuster

Children's Publishing Division

1230 Avenue of the Americas

New York, New York 10020

Copyright © 2003 by

Valorie Ann Fisher

All rights reserved, including the

right of reproduction in whole or

in part in any form.

Book design by Lee Wade

The text for this book is set in Filosofia.

Manufactured in China

First Edition

10 9 8 7 6 5 4 3 2 1

Library of Congress Cataloging-in-

Publication Data

Fisher, Valorie.

Ellsworth's extraordinary electric ears

and other amazing alphabet anecdotes /

by Valorie Fisher.

p. cm.

Summary: Photographs depict twenty-

six scenes, one for each letter of the

alphabet.

ISBN 0-689-85030-1

[1. Alphabet.] I. Title.

PZ7.F53485 El 2002

[E]—dc21

2001045899

ACKNOWLEDGMENTS

For their superbly silly suggestions in this enormously enjoyable endeavor, I give thanks to my son, Aidan; my mom and dad, Susan and Jim Fisher; Karen Hatt; Matt Mitler; and Barbara Ensor. I thank my daughter, Olive, for blithely believing she is obeying the "yust yooking" rule, and my husband, David, for his exceptional expertise in electrifying ears. And I give great gobs of gushing gratitude to Anne Schwartz and Lee Wade for their wondrous wealth of wit and wisdom.

LEBANON VALLEY COLLEGE LIBRARY

WITHDRAWN
LVC BISHOP LIBRARY

Alistair had an alarming appetite for acrobats.

Betty believed in a big but balanced breakfast.

Carleton's curious carousel captivated
the colorful carnival crowds.

Dot dreamed of driving a delightfully dainty dump truck.

E llsworth's extraordinary electric ears
were endlessly entertaining.

Fancy feathered fashions were favored
by Floyd's farm friends.

Gwendolyn's good-looking gorillas were great gardeners.

Holly was hugely happy in her humble handbag home.

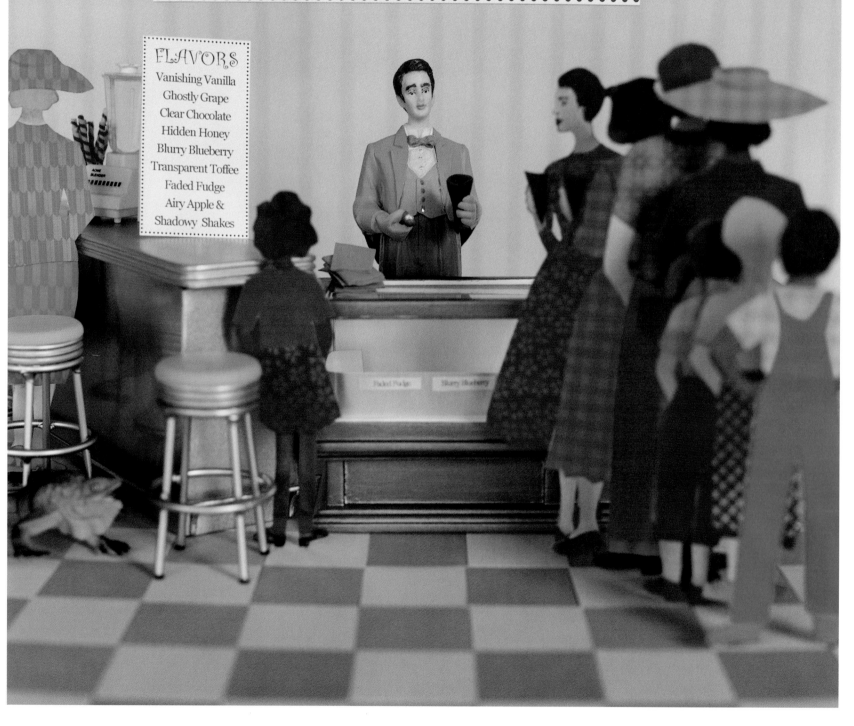

I t's incredible! Igor's invisible ice cream was irresistible.

Josie joined Judy on a jittery, jerky, jolly jaunt on her jackrabbit.

Kyle's kids kept kites in the kitchen.

Lucy's lopsided laundry line was loaded
with long and loopy letters.

Mario's mechanical moustache machine made many mistakes.

Nigel's nifty newspaper neckties were
nothing but a naughty nuisance.

Otis often observed ostriches on opening night at the opera.

P epita's pink paper parasols were particularly
popular with pirates. Perfectly puzzling!

Quentin quickly quieted the quibbling, quarreling, and quacking of the quintuplets.

Ruby was really rather remarkable at
refrigerator rocket repairs.

Supermarket-salad snacking was Stanley's summer sport.

Trust Trevor to tell you, typing on a trapeze was terribly tricky.

Uncle Upton's unusual utensils were unbreakable, unforgettable, and utterly useless.

V acationing in the valley of a violent volcano
was very invigorating for Violet.

Wilbur worked wonders with wallpaper.

Xanthia's X ray explained her exuberance.

Yates yelled, "Yippee for Yellow!"

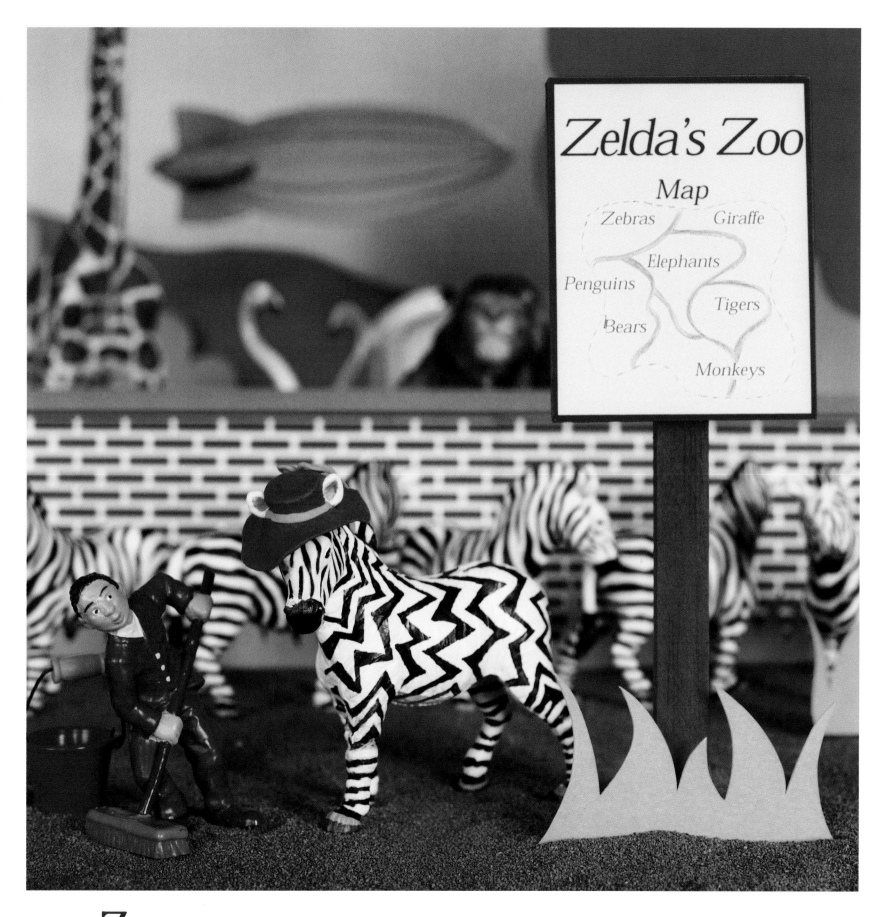

Zelda's Zoo
Map

Zebras Giraffe
Elephants
Penguins
Tigers
Bears
Monkeys

Zelda's zigzagged zebra was the zippiest at the zoo.

can you find these alphabet objects in each picture?

A

acrobat
airplane
alligator
apple
apple tree
ants
armadillo

B

baby
ball
ballerina
balloon
banana
baseball player
bat
bathing suit
beach
bear
beet
beverage
birthday cake
blue
blueberry
bottle
bread and butter
breeches
bucket
burger

C

cabbage
cap
camel
card
carnival
carousel
carrot
caterpillar
cheetah
chicken
chimpanzee
clock
cloud
clown
construction worker
corn
cow
cowboy
crab
crane

D

daisy
dice
dinosaurs
dirt
dog
dove
driver
duck
dump truck

E

ear
elephant
emu
envelope
eye

F

farm
feathers
fence
flashlight
foals
fowl
fox
frogs

G

gaggle of geese
galoshes
garden
gate
giraffe
goose
grapes
green

H

hair
handbag
handle
hat
head
heart
hoe
hog
hood
hoof
horse
hose
house

I

iguana
Igor's Invisible Ice Cream

J

jaguar
jewelry
jungle
Jupiter

K

kangaroos
ketchup
kettle

key
kitchen
kites
kitty
koalas

L

ladder
ladybug
laundry basket
laundry line
lawn
lawn mower
leg
lemon
lemon tree
letters
limb
lion
lizard
llama
locomotive
lollipop
LUCKY

M

machine
meerkats
monkey
moon
moose
moustaches
mouth

N

99
neck
necktie
nest
newspaper
nose
number

O

opera
opera glasses
ostriches
OTHELLO
owl

P

paintbrush
panda
pants
paper
parasols
parrot
pavement
pear
peas
pencil
penguin
people
PEPITA'S

pink
pirates
plates
purple

Q

Quail Quarterly, The
Queen Bee, The
QUIET
Questionable Quotes
Quilt or Quit?
Quintessential
    Quince, The
quintuplets
Quirky Queens

R

rabbit
raccoon
radio
rake
red
refrigerator rocket
rhinoceros
ribbon
robot
rock
roller skates
rooster
rope
ruler

S

salad
salamander
sand
seashell
shopping cart
shovel
skunk
snake
soap
soccer ball
soup can
spaghetti
spider
starfish
stegosaurus
strawberry
sugar
sunflower
supermarket
swimsuit/shorts

T

tail
teeth
tent
thumb
tiara
tiger
tightrope
tightrope walker
time
top hat
trapeze
trunk
tutu
two
typewriter

U

umbrella
underwear
unicycle
utensils

V

vendor
violin
Visiting Vesuvius
volcano

W

wagon
wallpaper
watering can
watermelon
wheel
wheelbarrow
white
window
window box
windowpane
wood

X

Xanthia
Ximenes
X ray
X-ray

Y

yard
yellow
yellow jacket
yo-yo

Z

zebra
Zelda's Zoo
zeppelin
zigzags
zookeeper